Party Problems

by C.L. Reid

illustrated by Elena Aiello

PICTURE WINDOW BOOKS
a capstone imprint

Emma Every Day is published by
Picture Window Books, an imprint of Capstone
1710 Roe Crest Drive, North Mankato, Minnesota 56003
www.capstonepub.com

Library of Congress Cataloging-in-Publication Data
Names: Reid, C.L., author. | Aiello, Elena, illustrator.
Title: Party problems / by C.L. Reid ; illustrated by Elena Aiello.
Description: North Mankato, MN : Picture Window Books, a Capstone imprint, 2020. | Series: Emma every day | Audience: Ages 5-7.

Summary: Eight-year-old Emma is excited about her best friend Izzie's birthday party, but she is also a little worried because she is deaf and communicates through sign language, and her Cochlear Implant does not work well in noisy crowds.

Identifiers: LCCN 2020001371 (print) | LCCN 2020001372 (ebook) | ISBN 9781515871804 (hardcover) | ISBN 9781515873112 (paperback) | ISBN 9781515871880 (adobe pdf)

Subjects: LCSH: Deaf children—Juvenile fiction. | Birthday parties—Juvenile fiction. | Best friends—Juvenile fiction. | Cochlear Implants—Juvenile fiction. | CYAC: Deaf—Fiction. | People with disabilities—Fiction. | Parties—Fiction. | Birthdays—Fiction. | Best friends—Fiction. | Friendship—Fiction.

Classification: LCC PZ7.1.R4544 Par 2020 (print)
LCC PZ7.1.R4544 (ebook) | DDC [E]—dc23
LC record available at https://lccn.loc.gov/2020001371
LC ebook record available at https://lccn.loc.gov/2020001372

Image Credits: Capstone: Daniel Griffo, 28–29
Design Elements: Shutterstock: achii, Mari C, Mika Besfamilnaya

Designer: Tracy McCabe

Printed and bound in the United States.
PA117

TABLE OF CONTENTS

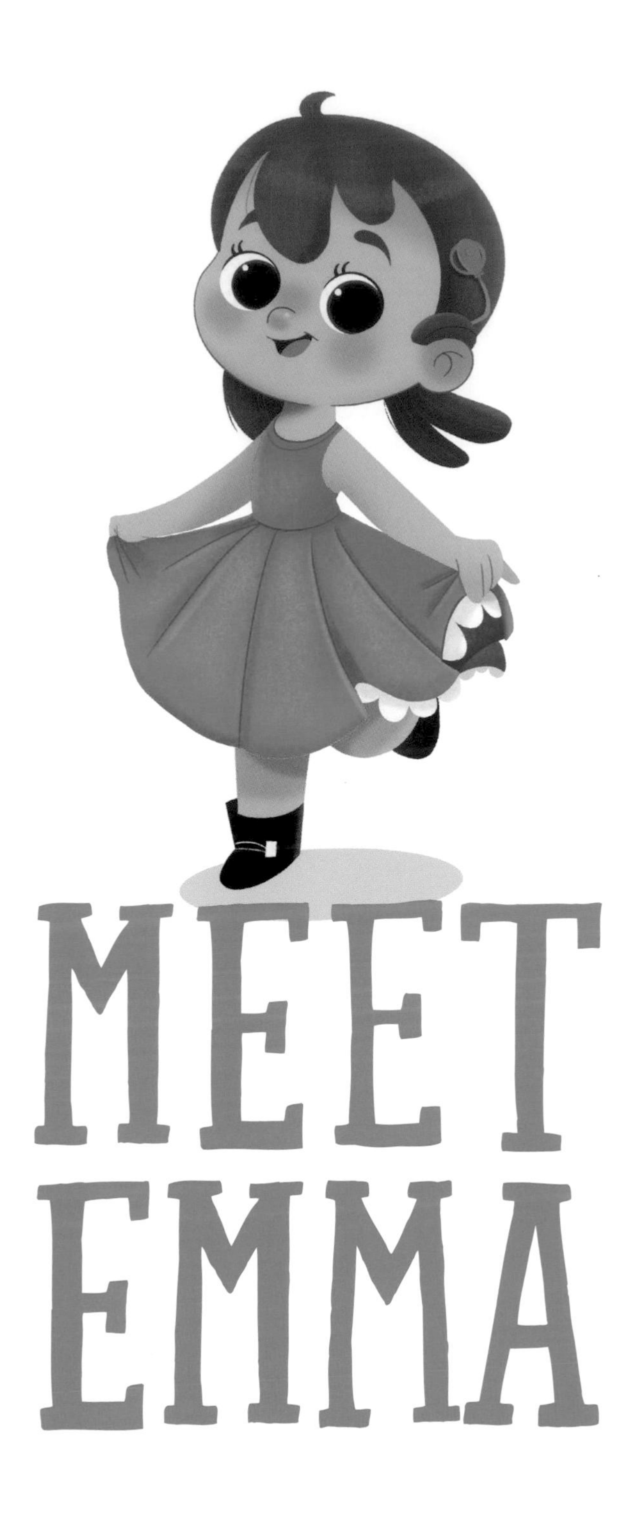
MEET
EMMA

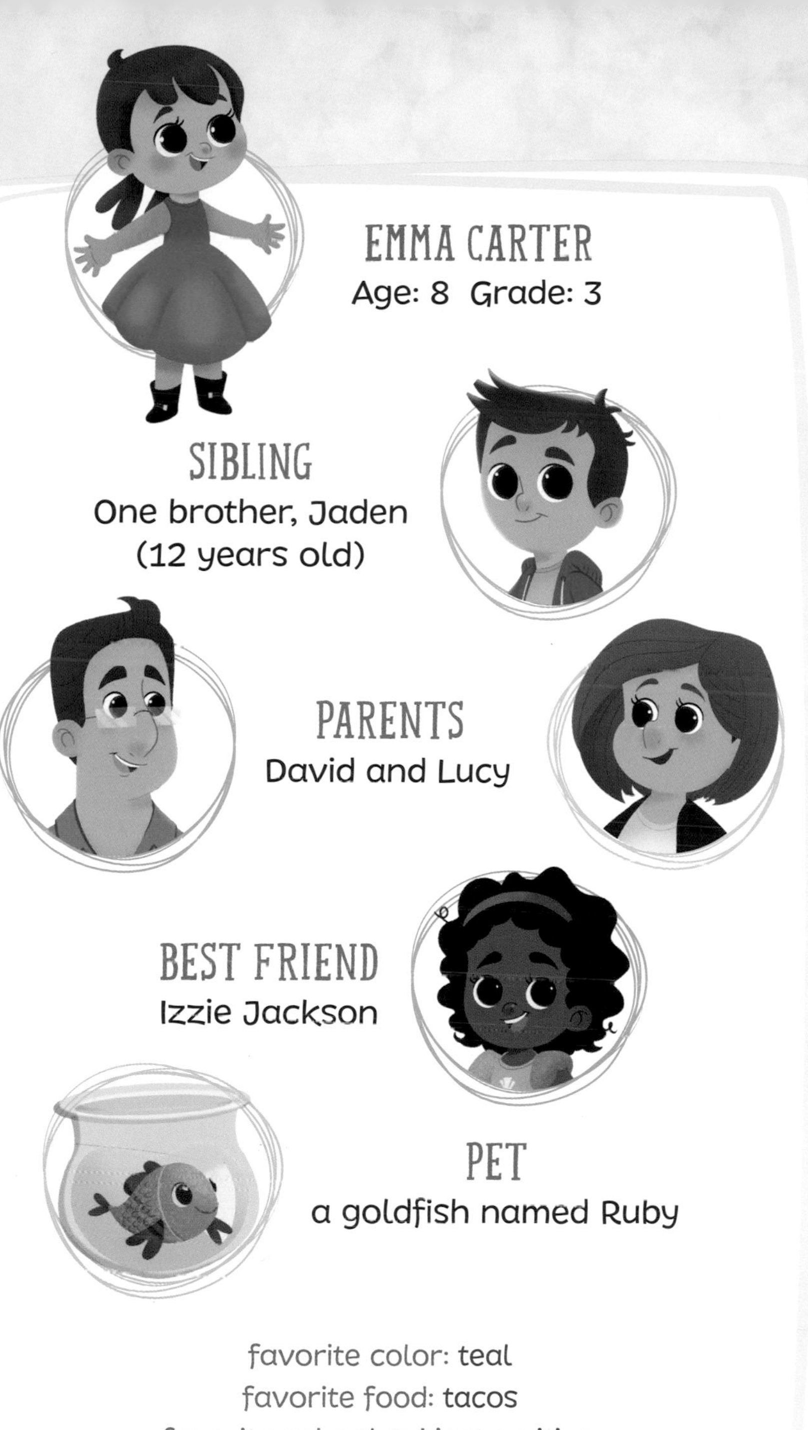

EMMA CARTER

Age: 8 Grade: 3

SIBLING

One brother, Jaden
(12 years old)

PARENTS

David and Lucy

BEST FRIEND

Izzie Jackson

PET

a goldfish named Ruby

favorite color: teal
favorite food: tacos
favorite school subject: writing
favorite sport: swimming
hobbies: reading, writing, biking, swimming

FINGERSPELLING GUIDE

MANUAL ALPHABET

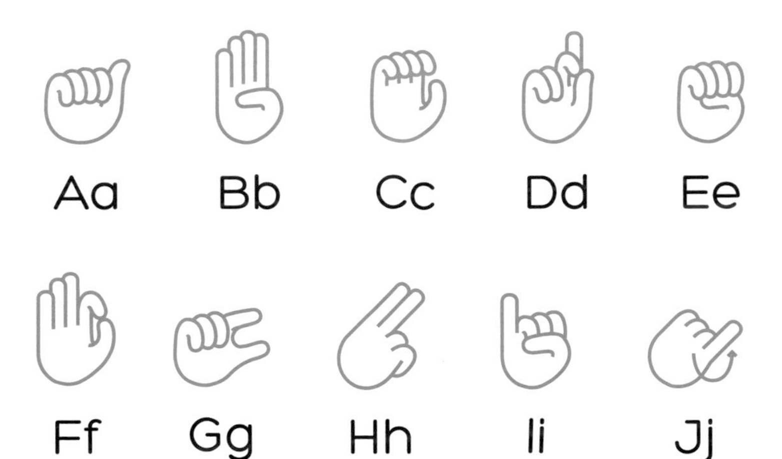

MANUAL NUMBERS

0 1 2 3

Emma is Deaf. She uses American Sign Language (ASL) to communicate with her family. She also uses a Cochlear Implant (CI) to help her hear.

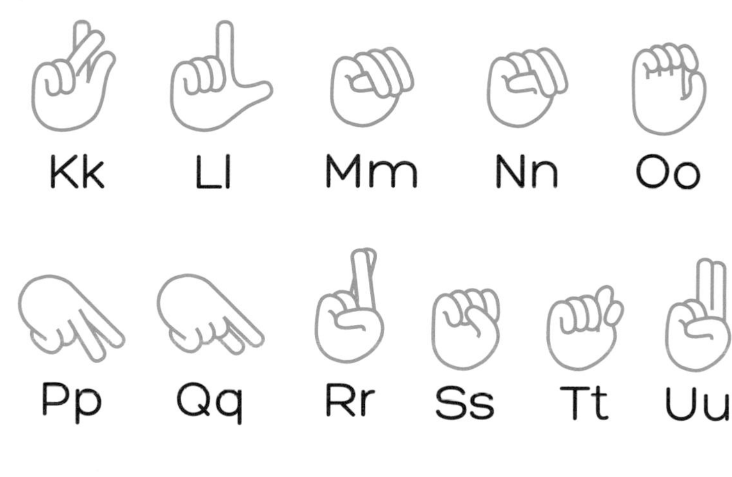

Chapter 1

Party Worries

Emma put on her Cochlear Implant (CI) and spun in her new dress. She was ready for Izzie's birthday party. Izzie was her best friend.

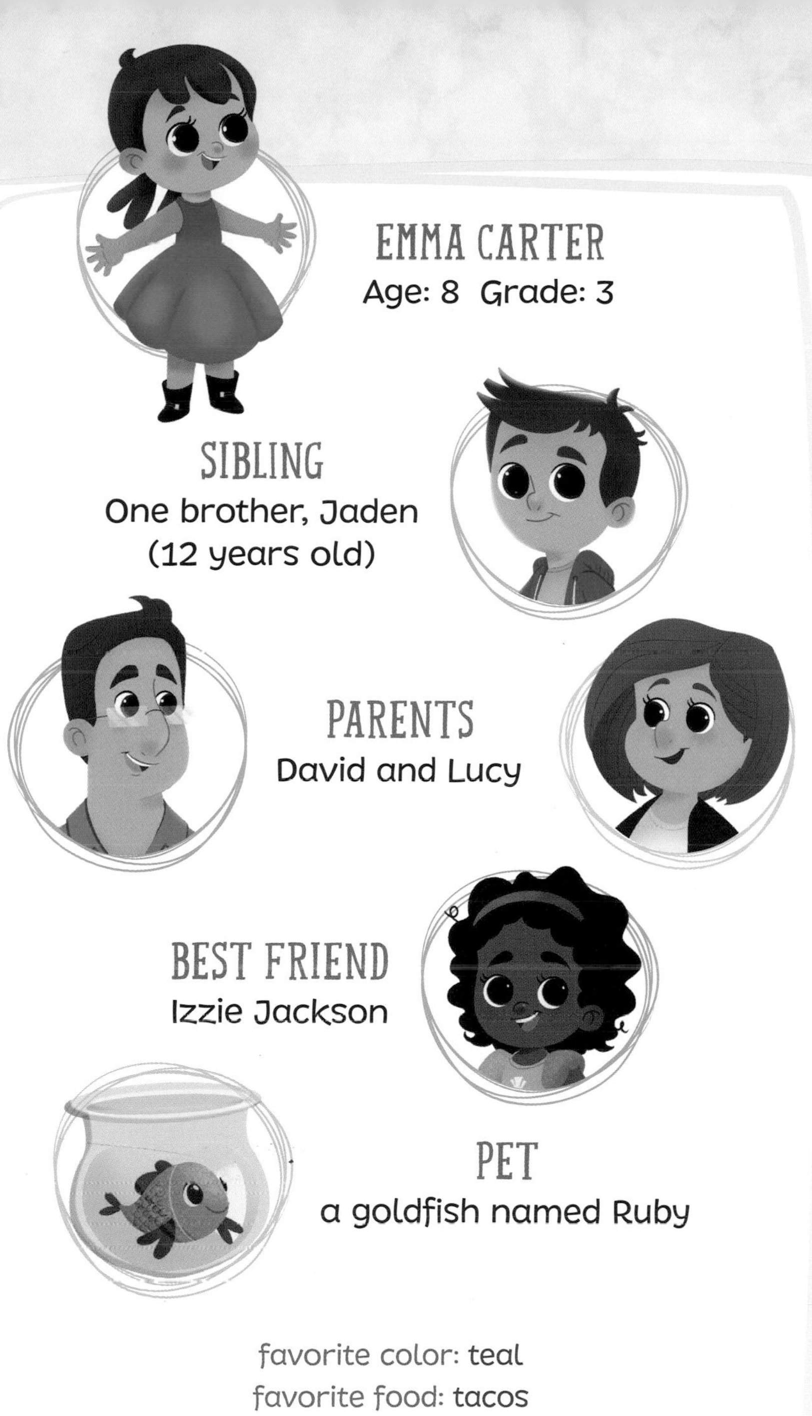

EMMA CARTER

Age: 8 Grade: 3

SIBLING

One brother, Jaden
(12 years old)

PARENTS

David and Lucy

BEST FRIEND

Izzie Jackson

PET

a goldfish named Ruby

favorite color: teal
favorite food: tacos
favorite school subject: writing
favorite sport: swimming
hobbies: reading, writing, biking, swimming

FINGERSPELLING GUIDE

MANUAL ALPHABET

MANUAL NUMBERS

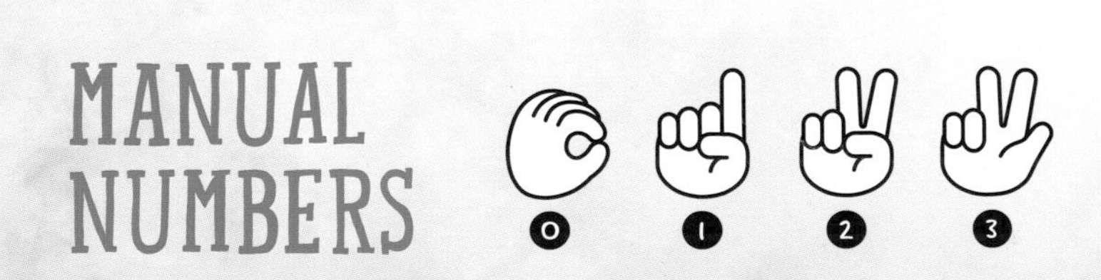

Emma is Deaf. She uses American Sign Language (ASL) to communicate with her family. She also uses a Cochlear Implant (CI) to help her hear.

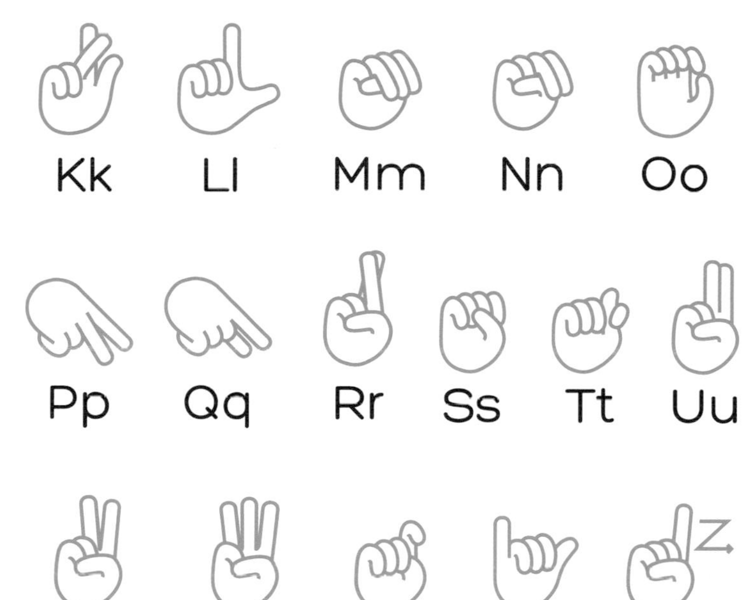

Chapter 1

Party Worries

Emma put on her Cochlear Implant (CI) and spun in her new dress. She was ready for Izzie's birthday party. Izzie was her best friend.

“Will everyone like this dress? Is it too fancy?” Emma asked Ruby.

Ruby was her goldfish. Emma loved talking to her.

"Do you think Izzie will like her gift?" Emma asked.

Emma had bought Izzie a pair of flippers. Her friend was crazy about mermaids. Emma and Izzie loved to swim.

“I’m so nervous. Will I know anyone at the party? Will I understand what people are saying?” she asked Ruby.

Emma looked in the mirror one more time. “Wish me luck!”

Emma went to say goodbye to Mom, Dad, and Jaden. Izzie lived just a few houses away. Emma could walk to the party by herself.

"I'm ready to go," she signed.

"Have fun," Dad signed.

"Bring me some cake," Jaden signed. Emma laughed.

"Are you nervous?" Mom signed.

"A little bit," Emma signed. "But I'm ready."

With one final wave, she walked out the door.

Chapter 2
Party Time

Emma skipped all the way to Izzie's house. When she rang the doorbell, Izzie answered right away.

“Hello,” Izzie signed.

Izzie knew sign language. She learned it when she met Emma two years ago.

“Happy birthday!” Emma signed, handing Izzie the present.

“I love your dress!” Izzie signed.

“Thank you!” One worry down.

Izzie's house was full of kids. It was really loud. Emma looked around. She didn't see anyone she knew. She started to worry again.

Emma heard squeals and laughter, but she couldn't make out any words. Emma pressed a button and changed the program on her CI. Maybe that would help.

A girl ran over to Emma and pointed at herself.

"Sarah," she said as she fingerspelled her name. "I'm Izzie's cousin."

"Nice to meet you," Emma signed.

"Nice to meet you too," Sarah signed back.

Izzie ran over and grabbed Emma's hand.

"Come on!" she said. "It's time to go outside and play the drop-the-bean-bag game."

In the backyard, the kids formed a circle. They cupped their hands behind their backs. Then they waited.

Izzie would put a bean bag into someone's hands, but whose?

The next second, the bean bag fell into Emma's hands. She spun around. Izzie ran past her. Emma chased Izzie around the circle and caught her arm.

"Ha! Ha!" Izzie fingerspelled, laughing. "You got me!"

Chapter 3

Mermaid Magic

After the game it was time for cake. Everyone sang "Happy Birthday." Emma sang and signed. Izzie blew out the candles and smiled. Everyone cheered!

The kids ran to the living room. It was present time! Emma couldn't wait for Izzie to open her gift.

She didn't have to wait long. Izzie opened Emma's gift first.

"Cool!" [fingerspelling: C-O-O-L] Izzie fingerspelled. "I love them! Let's go to the pool tomorrow. We will swim just like mermaids!"

"I can't wait!" Emma signed.

Izzie jumped up and swayed like a mermaid dancing under the sea. Everyone jumped up and joined in the mermaid dance.

When the party was over, Izzie gave Emma a huge hug.

"You really *mermaid* my day," Izzie signed.

"Well, we were *mermaid* for each other," Emma signed back.

They both laughed and hugged again. Sarah came over and joined the hug.

Emma left the party with a new friend and no worries. She couldn't wait to tell Ruby all about it!

LEARN TO SIGN

friend

1. Lock fingers. 2. Repeat with other hand on top.

happy

Make two small circles at chest.

birthday

Bring middle finger from chin to chest.

cake

Make C shape and slide down hand.

gift

Make X shapes and move forward twice.

party

Make P shapes and twist wrists.

thank you

Move hand away from lips.

GLOSSARY

Cochlear Implant (also called CI)—a device that helps someone who is Deaf to hear; it is worn on the head just above the ear

deaf—being unable to hear

fingerspell—to make letters with your hands to spell out words; often used for names of people and places

flippers—flat, rubber attachments that are worn on the feet to help someone swim

nervous—feeling worried

overwhelmed—feeling too much of something all at once

relieved—free of pain or worry

sign—use hand gestures to communicate

sign language—a language in which hand gestures, along with facial expressions and body movements, are used instead of speech

TALK ABOUT IT

1. Emma likes to talk to her pet fish. Why do you think she does that?

2. Emma has a lot of worries before Izzie's party. Talk about a time you felt nervous. What did you do to feel better?

3. Use the fingerspelling guide at the beginning of the book to sign your name.

WRITE ABOUT IT

1. Make a list of things you can do to make yourself feel better when you feel nervous or overwhelmed.

2. Emma makes a new friend at Izzie's party. Write about a time you made a new friend.

3. Pretend you are Izzie. Write a thank-you note to Emma for the flippers.

ABOUT THE AUTHOR

Deaf-blind since childhood, C.L. Reid received a Cochlear Implant (CI) as an adult to help her hear, and she uses American Sign Language (ASL) to communicate. She and her husband have three sons. Their middle son is also deaf-blind. Reid earned a master's degree in writing for children and young adults at Hamline University in St. Paul, Minnesota. Reid lives in Minnesota with her husband, two of their sons, and their cats.

ABOUT THE ILLUSTRATOR

Elena Aiello is an illustrator and character designer. After graduating as a marketing specialist, she decided to study art direction and CGI. Doing so, she discovered a passion for illustration and conceptual art. She works as a freelancer for various magazines and publishers. Elena loves video games and sushi and lives with her husband and her little pug, Gordon, in Milan, Italy.